THE REALLY AWFUL MUSICIANS

STORY AND PICTURES BY JOHN MANDERS

CLARION BOOKS

Houghton Mifflin Harcourt • Boston New York 2011

Clarion Books

215 Park Avenue South, New York, New York 10003

Text and illustrations copyright © 2011 by John Manders

Clarion Books is an imprint of Houghton Mifflin Harcourt Publishing Company.

www.hmhbooks.com

The illustrations were executed in gouache and colored pencil.

The text was set in 16-point Bodoni Classic.

Library of Congress Cataloging-in-Publication Data

Manders, John.

The really awful musicians / by John Manders.

p. cm.

Summary: In a faraway kingdom where music has been banned, an ever-increasing group of musicians
flees certain death, but when their terrible playing becomes too much for their horse, he teaches them
to play together by using musical notation.

ISBN 978-0-547-32820-1

[1. Musicians—Fiction. 2. Musical notation—Fiction. 3. Horses—Fiction.

4. Kings, queens, rulers, etc.—Fiction.] I. Title.

PZ7.M31247Re 2011

[E]—dc22

2011009638

Manufactured in China

LEO 10 9 8 7 6 5 4 3 2 1

4500315767

For my mom and dad

"Yuck!"

ONCE upon a time, in a kingdom amazingly far away, music sounded incredibly . . . well, bad. The king couldn't even stand to listen to his own royal musicians. One at a time they weren't so awful, but together they sounded horrible.

The king couldn't face another evening of it. "Enough! No more **LOUD**, soft, fast-fast-fast!, slo-o-o-o-o-o-ow, screechy, bellowy, terrible musicians! Hire me some mimes!" he thundered.

He decreed that henceforth, music would be banned throughout the kingdom,

and anyone caught playing music would be fed to the royal crocodiles.

The king's men-at-arms were everywhere, rounding up musicians. The royal crocodiles never had it better.

In an out-of-the-way village, little Piffaro
played a tune on his pipe: *pootpoot,*
pootpootpoot. Thum, thum thum thum
went his drum. But the royal men-at-arms
found his hiding place.

"Help me, Charlemagne!" Piffaro whispered to an old dray horse grazing nearby. (The horse's name wasn't really Charlemagne, but he liked the sound of it. He was proud of his mane.)

Piffaro vaulted onto his back, and off he rode into the night.

All night long he rode. Before dawn the next morning, Piffaro and Charlemagne were greeted by a sound that was almost too fast to hear.

deedlediddledeedledeedlediddledoodlediddledeedledeedle

11

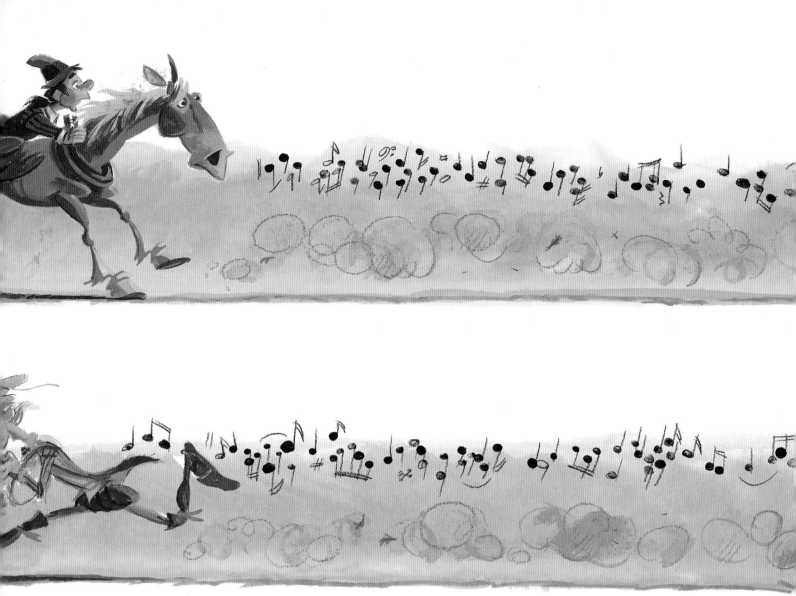

"I, Espresso, am the fastest musician in the kingdom!
Fast! Fast! Fast!" blurted the mandolin player.
"I can play a three-minute waltz in just under twelve seconds!"
   "We're escaping from the king's soldiers, if you want to come
with us," said Piffaro.

On they rode.

Piffaro's pipe went

pootpoot, pootpootpoot.

Thum, thum thum thum

went his drum.   Espresso's mandolin went

diddleedeedeedeedeepeleedleedoodleediddiddoodleedleedeedeepele

As the sun rose, Piffaro, Charlemagne, and Espresso noticed a teeny-tiny wee little tune that was almost too soft to hear:

Plinky-plinky plink-plinky-plink.

It was a little musician playing a tiny harp.

"I'm Serena the Silent," she whispered. "I hope I'm playing quietly enough."

"WHAT?" asked Charlemagne and Espresso.

"Come with us if you don't want to be an appetizer for the royal crocodiles," said Piffaro.

So on they rode.

Piffaro's pipe went

pootpoot, pootpootpoot.

Thum, thum thum thum went his drum.

Serena's tiny harp went

plinky-plinky plink-plinky-plink.

Espresso's mandolin went *deedlediddlediddle deedlediddlepootplediddlededlplediddlplpoodlepPlediddle.*

Around noon, they were nearly knocked over by sound waves.

WOOMPWOOMPAWOOMPOOMPOOMP!

The sackbut player paused for breath and said, "Congratulate me! I, Fortissimo, won the Loudest Musician in Boombardy Award this morning!"

"But Boombardy is at least three days' voyage from here," said Charlemagne.

"That's what makes it so impressive!" boomed Fortissimo.

"Jump in the cart," sighed Piffaro. And on they rode.

WOOMPWOOMPAWOOMPOOMPOOMP! went Fortissimo's sackbut.

Piffaro's pipe went pootpoot, pootpootpoot.

Thum, thum thum thum went his drum.

Serena's harp went plinky-plinky plink-plinky-plink.

Espresso's mandolin went deedlediddledoodlediddlepipipooopoooodiddledeedle.

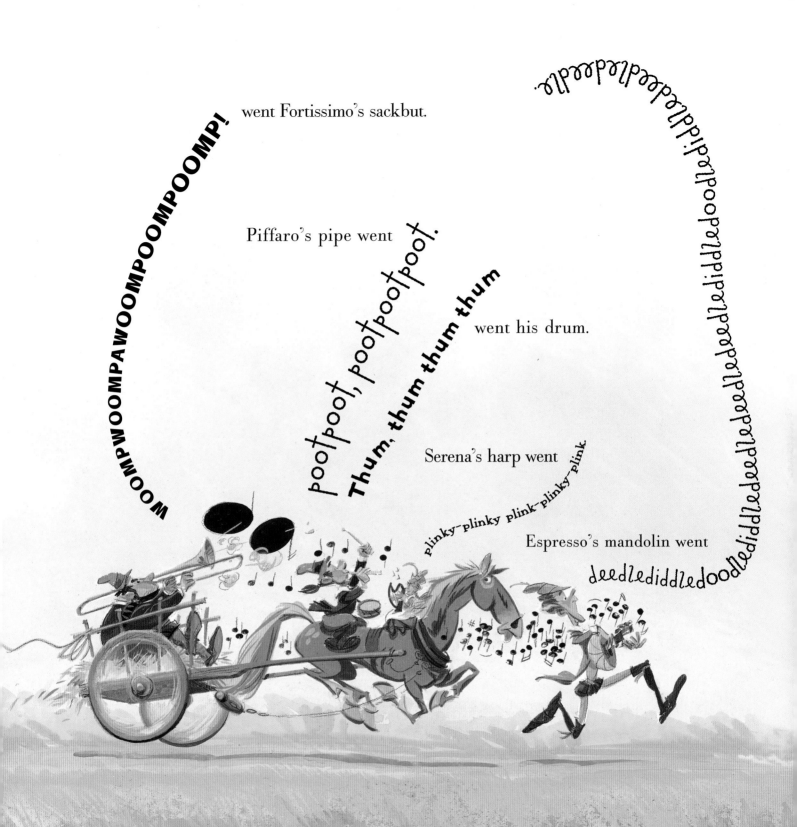

A few leagues down the road, they almost flattened the slowpoke inching along in front of them and going **bwaaaaaaaaaaa**

"Can't you go any faster?" asked Charlemagne.

"Nooooooooooooooooooooooo," replied Lugubrio, sadly. "I started playing this particular piece when I was a boy, and I'm just now starting the middle section."

"Well, climb aboard—the king's crocodiles are hungry already," said Piffaro.

'aaaaaaaaaaaaaaaaaaaaaaaaaaaaaaaaaaaaaaaaaaaaaa.

On they rode.

WOOMPWOOMPAWOOMPOOMPOOMP! went Fortissimo's sackbut.

bwaaaaaaaaaaaaaaaaaaaaaaaaaaaaaaaaaaaaa went Lugubrio's contrabass recorder.

Serena's harp went

plinky-plink

aaaaaaaaa

pootpoot, pootpootpoot. **Thum, thum thum thum** went his drum.

Piffaro's pipe went

pooPPPPPPPPPPPPiiddddddddddddlllldddeeeedddleedleedleedleedleedleedleedleedleeedleedleeddleediddlledoodleedleediddleedeedleedeedleedeedle

All afternoon they played as they rode. They played fast, slow, loud, and soft—all at the same time.

Espresso's mandolin went

plink-plinky-plink.

Finally, Charlemagne couldn't stand it anymore.

"Enough! You guys sound terrible! Why don't you all play together?"

The musicians stopped and looked at each other,

then at the horse.

Charlemagne drew five long lines in the dirt. "These lines are us riding along. I'll make hoofprints on the lines, to show high notes and low notes. The high notes will be up here, the low notes will be down here, and the middle notes will be in the middle. I'll mark time with this stick so you'll know when to play the next note."

They looked at Charlemagne's hoofprints and followed his stick.
While they played, each musician listened to the others. When they
all played together, the music sounded beautiful, for the first time ever.

And then the king's coach came barreling down the road.

"HALT!" cried the king. "Do I hear . . . *musicians?*"

Before the men-at-arms could grab them, Piffaro, Espresso, Serena, Fortissimo, and Lugubrio started to play—together.

The men-at-arms applauded. "Gadzooks, how lovely!" cried the king. "How would you like to play at my castle?"

"You won't feed us to your crocodiles?" asked Piffaro.

"Not if you play like that!" decided the king. "They can eat the mimes."

And so Piffaro and his friends became the king's musicians-in-residence, and beautiful music was heard everywhere from then on.

AUTHOR'S NOTE

SOME things in this story are almost true. When the real Emperor Charlemagne (which means "Charles the Great") came to power in A.D. 800, each choir throughout the empire (western and central Europe) sang music differently. They'd sing the same words of a hymn, but every church had a different tune. Charlemagne thought it would be a good idea if all the choirs sang from the same songbook, and so his minister, Alcuin of York, came up with the idea of musical notation—that is, writing down the notes of a tune. When the notes are written down, you can create a musical piece with more than one melody being played at the same time. It's notation that makes it possible for composers to write symphonies for large orchestras.

PIPE AND TABOR: The pipe is a woodwind instrument, and the tabor is a drum—a percussion instrument. One musician can play both at the same time. The pipe has only three holes, so the notes are fingered with one hand as the player blows into it. The tabor can be slung over the shoulder or hung from the waist, or even the wrist, and the player beats time with the other hand.

MANDOLIN: The mandolin is a string instrument, a member of the lute family. The strings are plucked, rather than bowed or strummed, so each note goes quiet very quickly. The player must pluck fast to get sustained, continuous music.

CONTRABASS RECORDER: A recorder is a woodwind instrument; a player blows into one end and achieves different notes by stopping the holes along its side with the fingers. A contrabass instrument has very low pitch—this one plays lower notes than other recorders.

SACKBUT: The sackbut is a brass instrument, the ancestor of the slide trombone. The French name for it was *sacqueboute*, meaning push-pull, which is what the player does with the slide part of the instrument to sound different notes.

HARP: The harp is a string instrument, the only one with strings perpendicular to the soundboard. They stand straight out from the soundboard, rather than being stretched across it, as on a mandolin.

This story was partly inspired by Piffaro, the Renaissance Band. If you'd like to hear some really good musicians, please visit their website at www.piffaro.com. If you're lucky, they'll stop by your town to give a concert.

No mimes were harmed in the making of this book.